the Naturalist's Handbook

Activities for Young Explorers

Lynn Kuntz

Illustrated by
Michael Moran

GIBBS·SMITH
P
PUBLISHER

To Val Worley . . . L. K.
To Kristin and Patrick . . . M. M.

VISTA GRANDE
PUBLIC LIBRARY

First edition
99 98 97 96 5 4 3 2 1

Text copyright © 1996 by Lynn Kuntz
Illustrations copyright © 1996 by Michael Moran

This is a Peregrine Smith Book, published by
Gibbs Smith, Publisher
P.O. Box 667
Layton, Utah 84041
Design by Z. Design

Note: Some of the activities suggested in this book require adult assistance and supervision, as noted throughout. The publisher and author assume no responsibility for any damages or injuries incurred while performing any of the activities in this book.

Library of Congress Cataloging-in-Publication Data:
Kuntz, Lynn, 1953-
    The naturalist's handbook: activities for young explorers/Lynn Kuntz; illustrated by Michael Moran.
    p. cm.
Summary: Provides basic facts about the natural world and includes participatory activities.
    ISBN 0-87905-728-9
    1. Nature study—Activity programs—Juvenile literature.
[1. Nature study.] I. Moran, Michael, 1957—ill. II. Title.
QH54.5.K85 1995
508—dc20   95-41122
                                               CIP
                                             AC

Contents

Becoming a Naturalist-Explorer

Have you ever imagined the excitement of being the first person to set foot in an uncharted land? Or dreamed of blasting off into space and discovering unknown worlds? If so, you have the spirit of an explorer.

Unfortunately, faraway voyages such as these probably aren't on your calendar just now. But you can, here and now, experience the thrill of discovery—day and night, during sunshine or rain, in winter, spring, summer, and fall— in an exciting, mysterious, and ever-changing universe as close as your own backyard!

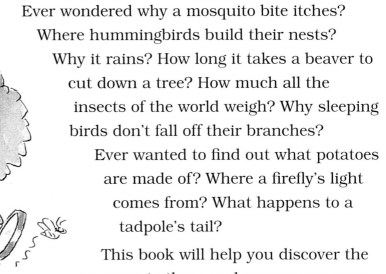

Ever wondered why a mosquito bite itches? Where hummingbirds build their nests? Why it rains? How long it takes a beaver to cut down a tree? How much all the insects of the world weigh? Why sleeping birds don't fall off their branches?

Ever wanted to find out what potatoes are made of? Where a firefly's light comes from? What happens to a tadpole's tail?

This book will help you discover the answers to these and many more questions. Take it with you when you hike through the woods, walk around the block, poke about a vacant lot, or just sit quietly on your own porch steps.

A Naturalist-Explorer Is a Detective

The skills detectives use (observing, questioning, measuring, comparing, and interpreting clues) are also used by naturalist-explorers to solve the mysteries of the world we live in. The only materials needed are everyday items you can probably find around your home.

Detectives take notes, and so should you. Write your questions, observations, and the facts you gather in the **Your Turn** sections provided in each chapter of this book. Uncover an answer? Draw a conclusion? Record it so you can share even the small, but important, details of your discoveries with others.

Opportunities and Responsibilities

What you do outside affects all the plants and animals that live there. Take care not to damage living creatures' food and water sources or places where they hide, make homes, and raise young.

Be gentle. If you pick up a worm, insect, or any other animal, be sure to put it back right where you found it. Pick flowers only from fields that have many flowers.

Ask permission before digging (even in your own yard). Respect the rules on public land. Don't litter. Leave every place just as you found it.

And don't forget: you'll impress (and probably surprise!) your parents by putting away tools and cleaning up after each project.

A naturalist explores plant and animal life.

Life is continually exciting and remarkable to those who take time to explore its mysteries. This is your world. Get to know it. The more you learn about the natural order of things, the better you'll understand and appreciate how YOU fit in!

Keeping a Field Journal

Your particular copy of *The Naturalist's Handbook* will be unlike any other book anywhere in the world—because you'll write and illustrate some of its pages as only you can.

Start each **Your Turn** section with the date and time. What's the weather like? Write, draw, or map the things you see and hear from day to day. Make sure you include lots of details. The more you can remember about what you've seen, heard, smelled, and felt, the better your chances of finding out more about it. Don't wait for rare sightings and unusual events; the word "journal" comes from a Latin word that means "daily."

There are so many kinds of plants, insects, and mammals that you won't be able to identify everything you see. Most adults won't either. Field guides can be a great help. They're available at most bookstores and your public library. Be sure you get guides with good pictures and language that you can easily understand (ask a salesperson or librarian for help).

Do include important seasonal sightings and signposts, such as birds flying south in the fall, the first winter snow, when dandelions begin to pop up in the spring, and what insects you spot on the first day of summer. You'll have fun comparing this year's notes with next year's calendar. When you run out of room in this book, continue your entries in other notebooks.

Your Turn might look something like this:

◯	
	March 14. It's windy. The sky is a clear, bright blue, and the sun's finally shining. I noticed the first tiny leaf buds on the big pecan tree. A mockingbird perched on one of the lower branches. He sang a song that sounded happy AND sad and reminded me of summer days. Wasps are swarming near the back door where the porch roof sticks out. I'll use the front! Our lawn is coming back to life—the grass still looks like straw, but there are lots of green weeds and even one dandelion flower.

ACTIVITY:
Sharpening Your Skills of Observation

Your first project is to learn to see, hear, feel, and smell more clearly than you ever have before. Practice wandering, watching, wondering, and listening for things others miss.

For starters, lie down under a tree. Close your eyes and tune into the chatter of birds; the scraping, scratching, humming, and buzzing of insects; the moans and sighs of the branches; and the songs the leaves sing.

Breathe deeply. What do you smell?

Run your fingers over the trunk. The bark is like a thick skin protecting the inside of the tree. Tiny cracks in the bark allow the tree to "breathe." Study the bark through a magnifying glass.

Roll over on your tummy (naturalist-explorers wear grubby clothes!) and look, really look, at the earth. Do you begin to get the feeling that up to now you've only scratched the surface?

Important discoveries are often noted in journals before they're shared anywhere else. The journals of Lewis and Clark, the famous nineteenth-century explorers, were for many years the world's most important source of information about the American West. You can even save flowers, leaves, and feathers between journal pages.

Your Turn: A Field Journal
Write the date and weather conditions with every entry. What have you seen? Smelled? Felt? Heard? Have any questions? Learned anything?

Plants Do Amazing Things

Did you open a door this morning? Sit at a wooden table? Eat cereal with sugar, or toast with fruit jelly? Did you drink orange juice or hot chocolate? Season your food with salt and pepper? Wipe your hands on a napkin? Read the comics?

Go lie down in the shade of a tree. Scoot around on a skateboard. Feed your cat. Ride a horse. Eat an ice-cream cone. Plunk a tune on a piano. Chew gum. Listen to birds sing. Cruise in a car. Go fishing.

Without plants you couldn't have done any of these things.

The cotton for your T-shirts and jeans comes from a plant. So does the paper for this book.

Did You Know?

- There are more than 380,000 different kinds of plants . . . SO FAR! Scientists think there may be just as many not yet discovered.

- Plants are the tallest living things known to man: California redwood trees top out at 360 feet—as tall as a 35-story building!

- Plants are the heaviest living things. Scientists estimate that the world's biggest tree weighs more than 2,750 tons. That's the weight of about 550 circus elephants!

- Plants are the oldest living things on earth. Lichens found in Antarctica have been around for 10,000 years. Imagine the invention of the wheel, the construction of the Egyptian pyramids, the birth of Christ, the first men on the moon, and virtual reality . . . all within one lichen lifetime!

Plants breathe and perspire, have plumbing systems that can pump thousands of gallons of water for hundreds of feet, can tell the time of day, and know which way is up and which is down. They make the soil fertile and hold it in place. Plants provide food for all living creatures (even meat eaters—you'll see!) and manufacture the very air that we breathe.

Question:
What does a plant have to do with a car?

Answer: Money may not grow on trees, but rubber for tires does!

Plant Potpourri

- The first living things on Earth were plants.

- Some plants are MANY times smaller than the period at the end of this sentence.

- Many plants know what time of year it is. They bloom exactly the same week every year, no matter what the weather is like.

- An average birch tree drinks 100 to 150 gallons of water every day during a warm summer.

- About 500 different types of plants eat animals.

An incredible variety of products come from plants: insect repellent, lubricants (oils) used in machines, and cosmetics (shampoo, lotion, and makeup). Almost half of all modern drugs and medicines are made from plants.

How Would You Like Your Meat, Sir?

Venus's-flytrap is a hungry, meat-eating (carnivorous) plant that grows wild in the swamps of North and South Carolina. The trap is made of two clamshell-shaped leaves with stiff, curved spikes that look like teeth. Each leaf has six sensitive "trigger" hairs. When an insect lands on the open leaf (and land they will—the flytrap lures them with its red color and irresistible sweet smell), it brushes the trigger hairs, and the trap snaps shut. Gotcha!

The unlucky insect struggles to escape. No way! The flytrap drowns it with a gooey juice. The juice gradually liquifies the insect (turns it into mush!), and the flytrap soaks it up.

In 8 or 10 days the trap slowly reopens. Out fall the body parts that were too hard to digest. Now the Venus's-flytrap is ready for its next victim!

Potted Venus's-flytraps are fed raw hamburger twice a week. Watch those fingertips!

✏ ACTIVITY: Dig In!

You can best begin your plant explorations down under—the ground, that is. Dig up a dandelion, a clump of grass, some clover, and a root vegetable (potatoes, carrots, or radishes, for example). Sketch the roots in **Your Turn** (page 21). Do they all look alike? Do any of the roots remind you of tree branches?

A rye plant can produce 385 miles of roots in 4 months—that's 3 miles a day!

Turn Sunshine into Food, Dew into Rain

Without electricity, smokestacks, assembly lines, or even a whisper of noise, leaf factories manufacture the food and oxygen that keep our planet alive.

All factories need machines. The machines of leaf factories are chloroplasts, little green cells that contain a chemical called chlorophyll. Sunshine is the power that runs the machines.

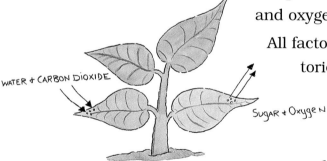

WATER + CARBON DIOXIDE

SUGAR + OXYGEN

Water + carbon dioxide = sugar + oxygen. This process is called **photosynthesis.**

Many scientists consider photosynthesis the most important chemical process in all of nature. After all, if plants didn't manufacture food, we'd all starve.

Water is pumped from the soil through the factory's pipes (the plant's roots, stems, and branches) to the leaves. Carbon dioxide gas from the air is sucked in through tiny holes, called stomata, on the back of each leaf.

Using these raw materials (water and carbon dioxide) the plant leaves in your yard may be making sugar right now!

What do you think happens to the food manufactured in the leaves of a plant? Watch how a growing plant changes. The stem becomes longer and thicker. New leaves appear. The roots grow longer. The food that plants make is what keeps them growing and healthy.

Leaves make more food than they need all at once. Some is stored until winter. Why do you suppose that's necessary? ➤ The extra sugar manufactured in carrot, potato, and beet leaf factories is carried in veins from the leaves to the stems to the roots, where it's stored. When you eat potatoes, beets, and carrots, you're eating food that the plants stored for winter.

(Here's a hint: the days are "shorter" in winter, with fewer hours of sunshine . . .)

Can you guess where the food made in the leaves of a corn plant is stored? In the kernels. Some of it may be ground into meal. When you eat crispy tortilla chips, you're eating food that was made in the leaves of a corn plant.

Where is the extra food made by pear trees stored? Tomato plants? Avocado trees? Bean vines?

Choose leaves from several different kinds of plants. Could each of them answer this want ad?

WANTED:
Thin, flat, green, full of tiny veins.

Answer: It's not getting enough water, sunlight, or carbon dioxide—the ingredients it needs to make enough of the right kind of food!

Question: When you don't get enough of the right kind of food, how do you feel? How do you look? What can you tell about a tired, pale plant?

ACTIVITY:

Want to see how water is piped through a plant? Choose a flower with a long, thick stem (daisies, carnations, and tulips work well). Slit the stem of the plant from the bottom up, 3 or 4 inches, so the stem is in two parts. Stand one part in a glass of water with red food coloring overnight. Stand the other part in a glass of water with green food coloring overnight.

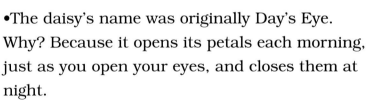

See for yourself how separate tubes inside the stems and branches pipe the red and green water all the way to the leaves.

Flower Facts

•The daisy's name was originally Day's Eye. Why? Because it opens its petals each morning, just as you open your eyes, and closes them at night.

•The biggest rose tree in America is 9 feet tall with a trunk wider than a yardstick. One hundred and fifty people can sit in its sweet-smelling shade!

•To help flying insects locate them, some plants advertise with special ultraviolet signs. These signs are invisible to humans except in photographs taken in ultraviolet light.

More than 250,000 plants are flowering plants. They come in all shapes and sizes and are the most advanced, adaptable, and successful of all plants on earth. Even though some look much more complicated than others, all flowers are variations of the same simple pattern.

Adaptable *means "able to change."*

All flowers are made of 4 circles of leaves at the end of a thick stalk.

1. The outside circle has small, usually green leaves called sepals. They protect the flower before it opens.
2. The next circle has brightly colored leaves called petals. Their job is to attract insects. (Why, you ask, would anyone want to attract insects? Wait and see!)
3. The third circle in has the stamens, thin stalks that produce powdery stuff called pollen. The stamens are the male part of the plants.
4. The circle in the very center has the pistils, sometimes partly hidden. They are the female parts.

Flowering plants include wheat, barley, corn, oats, and rice, all members of the grass family.

Fill in the blanks with these flower parts: petal, stamen, pistil, sepal, stem.

For a seed to be formed, a flower must be fertilized. For a flower to be fertilized, pollen from the male stamens of one flower must reach the female pistils of another flower. But how?

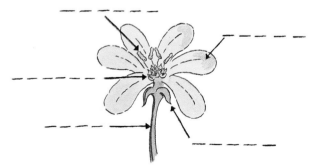

Can You Guess?

Did you know that many flowers close when it rains, to protect their delicate parts? When the sun comes out, they reopen.

1. What attracts insects to flowers?

Sweet nectar.

2. How is the pollen from the stamens of one flower carried to the pistils of another?

When insects dip into a blossom for a sip of sweet nectar, they brush against the stamens. Some pollen grains stick to their hairy bodies. When they fly to the next flower, some of the pollen falls off the insects and sticks to the pistils. This is called pollination.

3. What do you suppose the hardworking insects and birds that pollinate flowers get out of the deal?

Food. Butterflies, moths, hummingbirds, and bees get most of their food from the sugary nectar that flowers produce.

ACTIVITY:

Question:
Why should you NOT do this activity with a four-leaf clover?

Answer:
It's not good to press your luck.

You can save your favorite wildflowers by drying them in a simple flower press made of wood, cardboard, a thick newspaper, and straps (a couple of belts with adjustable buckles work well).

1. Cut well-formed, bright-colored blossoms (using scissors). Keep them fresh and undamaged by carrying them home in a shoebox lined with wax paper and damp cotton.

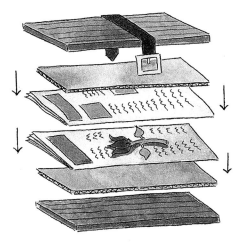

The final step is to remove flowers when dry. Save them in a scrapbook, picture frame, or glass-topped tray.

2. Find two flat pieces of wood (plywood is lightweight and easy to handle), 10 or 12 pieces of corrugated cardboard, and a stack of newspapers, all cut the same shape and size.

3. From the bottom up, stack a piece of wood, a piece of cardboard, and several sheets of newspaper. Place one or more flowers on the newspaper. Stack four or five sheets of newspaper on top of the flower(s) and continue stacking, alternating between flowers and newspaper. Add a piece of cardboard after every four flower arrangements. Finish the stack with the second piece of wood.

4. Press tightly together and bind with the straps. Store in a dry place.

Flowers have to do a lot more than look pretty. Their job, making seeds, is one of the most important jobs in the plant world. Why? Without seeds for reproduction, flowering plants would disappear from the earth. That would mean starvation for the rest of us.

The Wild Wandering Ways of a Seed

- Plants tuck their seeds inside fruits, nuts, or pods to protect them.

- Arctic lupine seeds have sprouted after being frozen in soil for more than 8,000 years.

- The world's largest seed is the coconut. Its thick husk is waterproof and light enough to float long distances on the water.

A tiny infant plant sleeps inside each seed, with the nub of its first root and shoot (the part of the plant that grows above ground) and enough stored sugar to feed it as it starts to grow.

But before it can grow, it must leave its parent plant. This usually happens in autumn and winter.

"Your mission is to spread out as far & wide as possible. It's every seed for itself, & anything goes. You may piggyback on birds, bees, & bats. You may stow away on trucks, cars & bike tires; trains, boats & boots. Have hooks & barbs? Use them!"

Question:
What would happen if all the seeds of a parent plant simply fell to the ground below?

Answer:
There wouldn't be enough light, soil, and water for all the plants that could grow from these seeds.

A man named George de Nestral noticed how seeds grabbed hold of animal fur. He made a fortune when he copied Mother Nature and invented Velcro.

Gone with the Wind

Some seeds twirl away in the wind on "wings." Some of the wings are round, some are long and narrow, and some are shaped like the blades of a tiny helicopter. Because the wing shapes of various kinds of seeds are different, they ride the wind in different ways.

Sycamore tree seeds head out into the world inside little round fruit balls that fall from branch to ground in early autumn (though you'll see some still hanging on all through the winter). When the ball breaks open, hundreds of seeds, each with its own little umbrella of silky hairs, sail away on the wind. Some may drop into rivers and be carried across continents.

Dandelions, willow trees, and cotton seeds are small and round with big, fluffy tops. When the pods open, the seeds float far and away, as if carried by miniature parachutes.

Beans, peas, geraniums, and violet seed pods shoot their seeds in all directions when they are ripe.

Still other seeds are equipped with hooks and stickers. Tickseed, teasel, and cockleburs catch on the fur of animals that brush against them. The animals then transport the seeds to all kinds of different locations.

The flowers of fruit bushes and trees hide their seeds in tasty fruits that birds and animals eat. After the fruit is digested, the seeds pass out of the animal in its droppings, perhaps hundreds of miles away.

Ever bitten into a green apple? It made you pucker, right? Can you see how the sour taste of unripe fruit protects the seed within? Here's a hint: a seed is mature and ready to go out on its own only when the fruit that protects it has grown ripe and sweet.

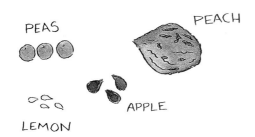

PEAS

PEACH

LEMON

APPLE

ACTIVITY: ✏️

Crack open an acorn, almond, walnut, pecan, or sunflower seed. How does the hard shell protect the infant plant? It keeps it from drying, drowning, or being eaten by animals.

Think of as many fruit trees as you can—apple, grapefruit, orange, date, peach, apricot, cherry, avocado, etc. Does the size of the seed or the size of the fruit have much to do with the eventual size of the plant?

Once water "unlocks" the stored food that a plant needs to start growing, the plant must get its shoot to the surface as quickly as possible. Why? Because a plant's supply of stored food is small. Once it reaches the surface, its own leaves can start making the food it needs.

Before a seed can grow into a plant, it must land on the right kind of soil with the right amount of sunlight. It must also have water.

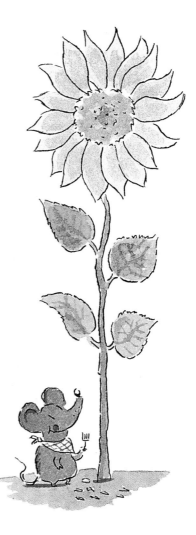

 ## ACTIVITY:

How does a newborn plant know which way is up? Its roots are equipped with gravity detectors!

Soak six dried beans in water overnight. Pour out the water the next day. Wad a paper towel into a clear glass. Place the beans against the glass (the paper towel will hold them in place) with each bean turned in a different direction. Moisten the paper towel each day, but make sure the beans aren't soaking in water.

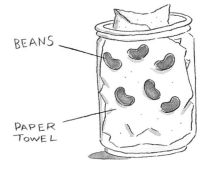

BEANS

PAPER TOWEL

Check the beans every day. When the roots appear, which way do they grow? Do they all grow in the same direction?

Medicine Plants

When European settlers first arrived in North America, there were more than 2,000 Native American tribes, each with its own system of herbal medicine. The pioneers were amazed to see herbs heal the Indians from injuries and illnesses that Europeans would have considered fatal.

What is a medicine herb? Any plant part (leaves, fruit, roots, flowers, bark, stems, or seeds) used to treat, cure, or prevent diseases.

Roots always grow down, and shoots always grow up, no matter which way a seed is turned.

The Ebers Papyrus is a scroll that was written in Egypt about 1600 B.C. It recommends more than 700 medicine plants, including peppermint, myrrh, and castor oil. It also prescribes placing a moldy piece of bread on open wounds. In 1928, over 3,500 years later, a scientist named Sir Alexander Fleming discovered that bread mold was a powerful antibiotic. This discovery led to development of the first modern "wonder drug"— penicillin.

ACTIVITY:

Place a piece of bread or fruit in a jar. Seal it with a lid. In a day or two, you'll see a fuzzy white, green, or gray mold on the food. The mold is an organism produced by a primitive plant called a fungus. The mold grew from spores (single cells produced by plants that are able to grow into new individuals) that floated through the air and landed on the food.

Gross? Maybe, but mold has saved countless lives.

Look at the mold through a magnifying glass. Does it look like other plants? In a few days, throw out the jar with the moldy food sealed inside. Some molds produce helpful medicines. Others can make you sick.

Your Turn: Plants Do Amazing Things
Make sure to record the date, weather conditions, and what you saw, heard, smelled, and felt in your explorations of plants.

Be sure to use more than your eyes. Sit still. What sounds do plants make? Do different plants make different sounds in the wind? In the rain? How do they feel against your fingertips? What do you smell?

Little Critters

How many insects can you think of? Flies, mosquitoes, lady-bugs, grasshoppers, butterflies, moths, crickets, ants, wasps, hornets, bees, fleas, beetles, gnats . . .

A single cabbage aphid can have 906 million TONS of descendants in one year. Fortunately, most of the eggs laid by the billions of insects in the world are eaten or destroyed before they make it to adulthood!

However many you came up with—20, 25, maybe even 50—you're not even close! There are 900,000 known species of insects in the world. And scientists say there are millions and millions of species not yet identified and named. So keep a sharp lookout!

A species is a particular group of animals that can mate and have babies together.

Red ants, for example, look a lot like black ants. But red ants can only mate and have babies with red ants. Black ants belong to a different species.

Bug Basics . . .

- There are about a BILLION BILLION insects in the world (that's 1,000,000,000,000,000,000—count those zeros)!
- More than half the world's living creatures are insects.
- There are a million insects for every person on earth.
- The insects of the world weigh 12 times what the people weigh.

How Vacant Is That Vacant Lot?

Between 500 and 2,000 insects can live in a single square yard of rich soil (not quite the size of a clothes dryer). Most are so small you can't see them without a magnifying glass or microscope.

Insect Check List

Although insects come in an incredible variety of shapes, sizes, and colors, adult insects are all alike in several ways:

- ✓ All have bodies divided into 3 parts: head, thorax, and abdomen.
- ✓ All have 6 legs.
- ✓ Each has 2 antennae (sense organs that feel and smell).
- ✓ Each has its skeleton on the outside of its body.
- ✓ Insects have no bones.
- ✓ All of them change forms (usually 4 times) during their lives. This is called metamorphosis.
- ✓ Many have 2 pairs of wings.

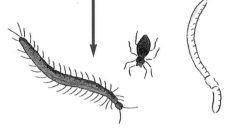

Earthworms, spiders, ticks, pill bugs, centipedes, and millipedes do not qualify as insects. Why?

form (n) the shape and structure of something

metamorphosis (n) a very great change

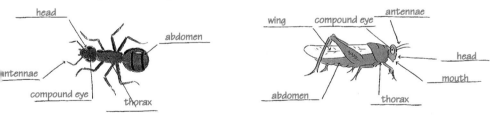

head

abdomen

antennae

compound eye

thorax

wing   compound eye   antennae

head

mouth

abdomen   thorax

Round and Round It Goes

If you saw a dark green caterpillar with yellow spots hunting for aphids on a rose bush, and a handsome, orange-and-black ladybug beetle flitting from one plant to another, you might think you were seeing two entirely different animals.

But if you hung out with either one long enough, you'd discover a fascinating cycle—the caterpillar would become a pupa,

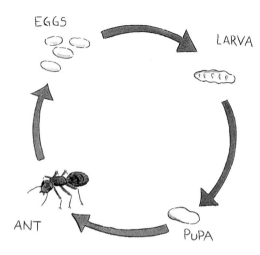

EGGS

LARVA

PUPA

ANT

A cycle is a circle, going on and on.

the pupa would turn into a ladybug beetle, the ladybug would lay eggs, and the eggs would hatch into a caterpillar, which would become a pupa . . . well, you get the idea.

Each form an insect takes has a special purpose:

1. egg: it contains everything needed to grow a new insect.

2. larva (wormlike or caterpillar stage): its job is to eat, eat, eat, and grow bigger and bigger.

3. pupa (cocoon stage): safe and quiet, the pupa lives off the fat it stored up in the larva stage and slowly turns into an adult.

4. adult: its only mission is to mate and lay a multitude of eggs. Then it dies. When the eggs hatch into larvae, the cycle of life starts all over!

ACTIVITY: Collectible Caterpillars

How many types of living larvae can you find? Look for caterpillars on leaves, twigs, and bark, and wormlike insects in corn, apples, and tomatoes.

Place each in a separate jar with a twig to climb on and plenty of whatever it was eating when you found it. Cover each jar with a nylon-stocking square and a rubber band. Number each jar. Write each number in **Your Turn**, followed by a description of the larva in that jar.

Keep the food supply steady and watch your larvae eat, eat, eat and grow, grow, grow.

When caterpillars first hatch from eggs, they have soft, moist skin. It soon dries and hardens. This is the caterpillar's exoskeleton. It provides shape and structure and protects the delicate organs inside its body.

A caterpillar will soon grow too big for its skin, and the skin will split and shed. Out crawls the caterpillar with another new, soft skin that was formed under the hard one. You'll see this happen several times to the larvae in your numbered jars. Note the dates in **Your Turn**.

When a caterpillar is big and fat enough, it's ready to become a pupa. It builds a protective case called a cocoon around itself.

Watch the larvae in your numbered jars wrap themselves up in cocoons. Back to **Your Turn**! Next to each jar number, note the dates its cocoon is completed. Your new pupae will sleep for weeks or even months.

Some insects bite or tear their way out of their coverings. Some ooze a liquid that melts the cocoon away.

When the adult insect first emerges, its wings are wet. It can't fly until they dry. When each of your captive insects is ready, let it go.

The larva of one North American moth eats 86,000 times what it weighed at birth in the first 2 months of its life. That's like a new-born human baby eating half a million hamburgers!

LARVA

COCOON

Syrup Sippers

Butterflies look so delicate that it's easy to picture a strong gust of wind sweeping them from the sky to the ground. But they're actually tough little critters, able to fly thousands of

Look for single monarch eggs on the backside of milkweed leaves (plants with milky juice and flowers growing in clusters). Look for a caterpillar with two tiny bumps on the head. The more milkweed it eats, the bigger it grows, and the bumps turn into long black antennae.

HONEYSUCKLE (WILD FLOWERS) THISTLE MILKWEED

miles over oceans and mountains.

Moth and butterfly wings are covered with scales so tiny they look like colored dust. These scales give them beautiful wing patterns.

Even lightly touching a butterfly's wings could damage the scales and ground it. Unable to fly, it would soon die.

ACTIVITY:

Get up close and personal with butterflies with these simple tips:

1. Hunt butterflies on sunny, warm days, especially after spells of cool, cloudy weather.

2. Move with the sun at your front, so you don't make a shadow.

3. Hang out in flower gardens and overgrown fields with lots of milkweed, wildflowers, and thistle.

4. If you're slow and sly you can get close enough to watch them sip nectar through a long mouth tube—sort of like a soda straw! Notice that when the butterfly's not sipping, the tube is coiled.

Each autumn, millions of bright orange-and-black monarch butterflies fly over a thousand miles from their summer homes in Canada to their warmer winter homes in Mexico.

One female monarch butterfly was nabbed and tagged in Canada, then set free. She was recaptured in Mexico—5 months and 21,333 miles later!

Why aren't migrating monarchs gobbled up by migrating flocks of birds? A little black spot on each hind wing has an odor that birds can't stand!

Beetles: The Good, The Bad, and The Ugly

Beetles are the largest insect group in the world. In fact, there are more species of beetles (around 350,000) than any other kinds of animals. You can find them on tree bark and leaves, in the water and soil, under rocks and dead leaves and rotting logs—just about anywhere!

GO AHEAD MAKE MY DAY!

You'll recognize beetles by the shiny shells on their backs. The shell is actually a pair of hard front wings folded back over soft flying wings.

The Good:

Everybody loves the pretty, perky, ladybug beetle, but most especially farmers and gardeners. Why? Because ladybugs protect crops and ornamental (pretty to look at) plants by eating the kinds of insects that destroy them.

Ladybugs lay tiny, yellow eggs in clusters on leaves.

A ladybug's bright colors protect it from bug-eating birds. In the "body language" of nature, bright colors say, "Stay away! I taste terrible!"

Scarab dung beetles are also good beetles. They fertilize the soil by collecting and burying the dung (droppings) of other animals. Scarab beetles even lay their eggs in the buried dung. When the eggs hatch, what do you suppose the larvae eat? Dung!

Long ago some people thought toothaches were caused by little worms drilling through the root. Their solution? Placing a beetle in the mouth to eat the worm!

PIERCING TUBE   BLOOD VESSEL

Why does a mosquito bite itch? The poison pumped into your skin when a mosquito bites you is actually a chemical that keeps your blood from thickening, the way it usually does when you're cut. Your body reacts to this chemical by swelling and itching.

Sexton beetles get rid of dead, decaying, and sometimes disease-spreading small animals. They do this by scooping a hole in the ground beneath the animal's body and dragging it in. Females lay eggs in the rotting flesh. When they hatch, what do you suppose the larvae eat? The rotting flesh.

The Bad:

Colorado beetle larvae eat whole fields of potatoes. This beetle will lie on its back, legs and antennae folded, and play dead when threatened.

Bark beetles burrow beneath the bark of trees, often spreading diseases that kill whole forests.

June bugs are dark, shiny beetles whose blind, hungry, yellowish white larvae gobble the roots of certain types of grass, frequently wiping out entire lawns in a single season.

The Ugly:

Bloody-nosed beetles gross out enemies by squirting stinky red juice from their mouthparts. It looks like they have bloody noses!

Male stag beetles have ferocious, branching mandibles (jaws), which they use as weapons in fights with other stag beetles.

Flies: Who Needs 'Em?

The common housefly is one of the biggest troublemakers of the insect world. Flies spread germs that make millions of people sick each year.

Each of a fly's six legs has four joints. The outermost joints are the feet. A fly's hairy, padded feet are coated with a sticky substance. This is why flies can walk upside down on the ceiling.

Flies eat and lay eggs in rotting garbage, dead and/or diseased animals, and rotting manure. Germs from these things stick to their feet. This is why you shouldn't eat unrefrigerated, unwrapped, or unwashed food. Flies have probably landed on it.

Fly Odds and Ends:

- Flies have two compound eyes and three simple eyes.
- Two small knobs behind a fly's two flying wings help it keep its balance while flying.
- Ever wondered how flies know just when dinner's served? Their antennae have an incredibly keen sense of smell.
- Why do flies rub their legs together? To clean off some of the stuff that sticks to their legs and feet.

ACTIVITY:

Study the life cycle of flies. Put a peeled, ripe banana in a quart jar. Leave it uncovered for several days. As soon as there are 8 to 10 fruit flies flitting around inside the jar, cover the top with a piece of nylon stocking and a rubber band. Keep the jar covered for 3 days, then let the flies go (outside!). Cover the jar with the piece of nylon stocking again.

Look inside the jar each day. Soon you'll see maggots, the larvae of flies, crawling around. Before long, the maggots will become sluggish and enter the pupa stage. Finally a new generation of flies will hatch.

Question:
Can you explain what happened? How did the fruit flies discover the banana in the jar?
Answer:
Sense of smell

Question:
Where did they lay their eggs?
Answer:
On the banana

Awesome Ants

Ants live everywhere you can imagine, except the South and North Poles and the tip-tops of the world's very highest mountains.

Whether at home in a concrete city or in the jungle tropics, ants live together in organized communities called colonies. Three types of ants live in each colony: the queen (the largest ant), male "princes," and hundreds, thousands, or even a million female workers. Each has a certain job to do. If any job is left undone, the colony will soon die.

It all begins with the queen, whose job is to lay eggs. A new ant colony is begun when a freshly hatched queen flies from her birth colony, mates with one or more male princes, and burrows into the ground (or a rotting tree) to lay her eggs.

The new queen takes care of the first batch of eggs all by herself, making sure they are clean and fed throughout the larvae

Body Language

When the queen has something to say, her body produces a special juice that contains a message. Workers lick the juice from her body and pass it, mouth to mouth, to all the ants in the colony. This is how the workers know what she wants them to do.

Worker ants are all females. They have no wings and can't fly. Some are engineers. They build the various rooms, storage areas, bridges, and tunnels of the colony. Others are nursery workers. They take care of the eggs the queen lays. A different set of caretakers feeds and bathes the larvae and pupae.

Janitor ants keep the colony clean. Scout ants scurry far beyond the colony's boundaries, searching for food. Food-gathering ants carry whatever the scouts find back to the nest, where other ants will store it or prepare and feed it to the rest of the colony. Soldier ants give up their lives in defense of the colony.

and pupae stages. When they reach adulthood (9 months after the eggs were laid), the ants go to work.

The worker ants' first job is to leave the nest and find food for the queen (who has been inside all winter with nothing to eat). Then they begin digging rooms and hallways under the ground.

The queen's only job for the rest of her life is to let the workers pamper her while she lays eggs, eggs, and more eggs.

The male princes' only assignment is to mate with the queen. Princes hatch in spring, mate in summer, and then die.

ACTIVITY:

Look for ant colonies in your yard. Watch the ants pulling, pushing, and carrying twigs, pieces of plants, and food (including other insects) to the nest. These loads can weigh 20 times what the ant weighs. Watch them work together to move something too heavy for one to move by herself.

Scatter a few grains of sugar in the pathway of some ants. Sprinkle a few grains of sand. Then drop a few blades of grass. Look through a magnifying glass to see what they do.

Look for trails around the ant nest. Trails lead to steady sources of food, friendly neighborhood ant colonies, and the ant cemetery.

Ants spend the cold winter months huddled together deep in their nests. On warm sunny days, the workers come out to soak up some sun. They "sunbathe" until their bodies warm up to between 86 and 104 degrees Fahrenheit. When they go back into the nest, their body heat warms up the whole colony.

Special attendants feed and clean (by licking) the queen.

ANT STINGS CAN BE DANGEROUS! Do not lift stones or dig into a nest without an adult's permission. Stay away from FIRE ANTS.

Starlight, Star Bright, First Bug I See Tonight . . .

Nighttime Activities:

1. Check all the outside lights around your house and garage. Which insects seem to love the light?

2. Place a flashlight outside at night under a white sheet. Wait to discover who "sees the light."

3. Dig a hole in the ground the size of a soup can or jelly jar. On a clear night, when no rain is expected, set an empty can or jar in the hole so the surface of the ground is even with the can's top rim. Drop a small bit of meat or hard-boiled egg to the bottom for bait. Check first thing in the morning to see who "dropped in."

4. Note the results of each of these activities in **Your Turn**

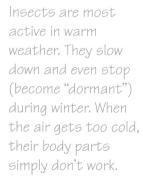

ACTIVITY:

Bet you didn't know you could tell the temperature by counting the number of times a cricket chirps!

Capture a cricket and put it in a jar. Cover the top of the jar with nylon stocking and a rubber band (or a lid with airholes).

Count how many times the cricket chirps in 15 seconds. (You can count "one thousand one, one thousand two" all the way to fifteen. But a watch with a second hand is more accurate.) Add 40 to the number of chirps. This is the temperature in Fahrenheit degrees. Do it more than once for accuracy.

Insects are most active in warm weather. They slow down and even stop (become "dormant") during winter. When the air gets too cold, their body parts simply don't work.

Nightlighters:

You may have seen fireflies, or lightning bugs, winking and blinking on warm summer nights. What most people don't realize is that every twinkle has a time and reason.

Why do fireflies light up? To attract mates. The lights you see flitting and bobbing against the night sky belong to the males. Females have short wings and can't fly. Lights flashing from the ground belong to them.

Each species of firefly (there are over 2,000!) communicates in its own secret code. When a female spots the inviting glow of a male from her species (she'll know he's "her type" if his flashes last just the right amount of time with just the right pause in between), she'll answer with a glow even brighter than his. When he flashes, "Where are you?" she flashes back, "Over here." He'll follow her flashes until he finds her.

One tricky, firefly-eating beetle can imitate a firefly's flashing code. When a true firefly responds, the sly predator beetle attacks.

As soon as summer arrives, catch some fireflies in your bare, cupped hands. Not to worry—they don't bite or sting!

ACTIVITY: Can you speak firefly?

See if you can "crack" a firefly code. Find a comfortable place to sit outside, and study the pattern of a male firefly's flashes (the ones in the air). How many times does he flash in one minute? How long do the flashes last?

Pretty scary! The main difference between tarantulas and other spiders is size.

Now see if you can copy the pattern with a flashlight. The kind of light you use isn't important. What is important is that you copy exactly the length of each flash and the time in between flashes.

The females of most species respond to the signals of prospective mates in exactly 2 seconds. Watch for a flash from a male firefly. Get down on the ground and flash him back with your flashlight, after exactly 2 seconds. Does he flash you again?

What's Special About Spiders?

- Spiders are NOT insects.

- Spiders have fangs that are filled with poison! (But only a few species' fangs can pierce human skin.)

- Some spiders never spin webs. Others spin them all underwater.

- Most spiders have 8 eyes but very poor eyesight.

- Spiders are arachnids. Unlike insects, they have 8 legs, no wings, and only 2 body sections: the cephalothorax (head and thorax combined) and abdomen. They live in all kinds of habitats, in every climate.

Yeah, spiders look mean. No wonder most people don't want them around.

But wait a minute. Most are harmless to humans. The fact is, we couldn't live without them. By catching flies, mosquitoes, and other insects that carry diseases, spiders protect human beings. And if it weren't for spiders, the insect population would grow so large and wipe out so many food crops that many people would starve.

Spiders make liquid silk, called gossamer, from glands in their abdomens. It flows out through tiny tubes, called spinnerets, at the tip of the spider's abdomen. As soon as it hits the air it becomes solid.

Spiders make different kinds of silk to be used in different ways. The spokes of a web are spun with very sturdy silk to support the web's structure. The threads that spiral around the spokes are sticky, so they can catch and hold insects. The silk for the cocoons that cradle a spider's eggs must be able to protect what's inside from the sun and the rain.

To spin a thin thread of silk, a spider holds its spinnerets close together. To spin a thick strand, it spreads the spinnerets apart. Some spiders spin sheets of silk by combing together thread from all the spinnerets with their back legs.

ACTIVITY:

Watch a common garden spider spin a wheel-shaped orb web. Notice how the spider settles down to wait when the web is complete. Where does it wait? Why?

When an insect wanders into the spider's web and is caught, it struggles to get away. The movement of the web tells the spider that dinner is served. The spider rushes out, paralyzes the trapped insect with a bite from his poison-tipped fangs (which turns its insides to liquid!),

Nearly a mile of silk thread goes into a cocoon.

Why don't spiders get stuck in their own webs? For one thing, they have the right kind of feet (custom-made for traipsing around on silk lines). And their legs are coated with oil. But most importantly, each spider knows which threads in its web are sticky, and which are "safe."

and then wraps it in silk to eat (or rather drink) later.

ACTIVITY:

Spiders are born knowing how to spin webs; their first is as perfect as their last.

Save an orb web on a piece of poster board (or cardboard). You'll need a small can of dark-colored spray paint, a piece of light-colored poster board, scissors, and the help of an adult.

Choose a time when there's no wind. Find a perfect orb web (gardens are great places to look). Shake the spider who lives there into a box or jar and turn it loose nearby.

Gently spray both sides of the web with paint. Quickly, before the paint dries, place the poster board against the web. Take care that all parts of the web touch the poster board at the same time. Use the scissors to cut the long silk threads that stretch past the main part of the web.

Lay it flat until it's completely dry. Write the date, type of web, and where you found it on the bottom of the poster board.

What Do You get when you cross A Rabbit AND A Spider?

A hareneti

	Your Turn: Little Critters
○	

Bigger Critters

You belong to a group of bigger critters called mammals. Other mammals include dogs, cats, cows, horses, rabbits, foxes, squirrels, giraffes, bears, raccoons, beavers, mice, elephants, bats, seals, and even whales. Once you've read about mammals, add others you think of to a list in the **Your Turn** section.

Would you believe?

• Only 3 out of every 100 living animals are mammals.

• Humans live longer than any other mammals. Elephants are next, sometimes reaching the ripe old age of 70 or 80.

• The loudest mammals are large whales. Their calls can be heard in the water hundreds, perhaps thousands, of miles away.

• Some opossums sleep for 19 out of 24 hours.

• The word raccoon means "he scratches with his hands" in the Algonquin Indian language.

Mammal Musts

All mammals . . .

✓ are warm-blooded. In other words, the temperature inside their bodies stays about the same, no matter how much the temperature outside changes.

✓ have some hair on their bodies.

✓ drink milk produced in their mothers' mammary glands when they are babies (mammary . . . mammal—do you see any connection?).

✓ have lungs and breathe air.

✓ have bones, including a backbone.

What are some of the things people most need to live? What about other mammals? A warm, safe place to sleep, plenty of wholesome food to eat, clean water to drink, and a healthy place to raise children are musts for all mammals (humans included).

More About Mammals

One common group of mammals is called rodents. Rodents gnaw their food with long, sharp front teeth. Mice, rats, hamsters, gerbils, beavers, marmots, and squirrels are all rodents. Because rodents' teeth keep growing and growing, they must keep gnawing and gnawing! What do you suppose would happen if they didn't?

Squirrels learn where to bite different kinds of nuts so they'll split open easily.

Rabbits and hares also gnaw their food, but they're NOT rodents. They have two extra front teeth that rodents don't have. Can you guess how overheated rabbits and hares release body heat? Through their long ears!

Mammals that hunt and eat the meat of other animals are called carnivores. They have to be strong and fast to catch and kill. Bears, coyotes, lions, tigers, wolverines, foxes, wolves, dogs, and cats are carnivores.

Although most human beings are carnivorous, some people think it's healthier and more humane, or kind, to be vegetarian, eating only fruits, vegetables, grains, and other plant parts.

Horses, cows, deer, goats, sheep, antelope, pigs, camels, and giraffes are hoofed mammals. They're all plant eaters.

CAMEL   ANTELOPE   HORSE

Hooves are very large toenails.

Deer are shy mammals. Their senses of sight, smell, and hearing are keen. Their safety depends on how still they can stand or how quickly they can run when their senses warn them of danger.

Have you ever seen a deer standing as still as a statue, except for its ears? Deer pick up sounds by turning their ears without turning their heads. Look for other mammals with ears that move individually toward sound.

When Petting's a Problem . . .

Whitetail fawns are trusting and can easily be taught to accept food from people. Some people encourage them to visit their yards and homes from nearby woods. Some even pen them up.

But cute little fawns grow up to be big deer. Few fences are high enough to hold them. Sooner or later, they'll be back in the fields and forests.

Deer that were tamed when young have little chance of surviving. Shyness and fear of humans are a deer's main protection against highways and hunters. This is why many states have laws against people making pets of deer.

Home Is Where the Hole Is

Mammals make their homes wherever they can be warm, safe, and well-fed. For some, that means a hole in the ground. For others, a treetop nest provides all the comforts of home. Still others live in salty ocean swells.

Rabbits hollow out nests in thick, low bushes, lining them with soft grass and their own fur. They also take over the abandoned holes of other mammals, turning them into large, many-tunneled, underground burrows called warrens. Rabbits spend most daylight hours in their nests, coming out at night to eat. When a rabbit senses danger, it thumps its back feet on the ground to warn others to dash toward escape routes, or "bolt" holes.

Raccoons live where there are plenty of trees and water. After fishing (for crayfish, clams, fish, and frogs) and foraging (for nuts, berries, corn, and fruit), raccoons curl up to sleep in hollow logs, tree holes, attics, and even chimneys!

Raccoons also love tasty garbage—especially if it smells like chicken or fish.

Squirrels spend the cold months curled in nests in high tree holes. In summer they move to the breezy treetops. Look for a messy mass of twigs, leaves, and bark (comfortably lined with grass, thistledown, and feathers) to find a squirrel home.

Deer bed down in deep forest shadows near the meadows where they graze. Look for a small area of flattened foliage. Many deer migrate to remote, higher ground in summer and back to lower, gentler lands in winter.

A fawn's dappled coat makes it almost impossible to see against the sun-speckled leaves of the forest floor.

Bears sleep away much of the winter in caves or rocky clefts. But they're not true hibernaters. Because their body temperatures fall only a few degrees, they may wake on warm winter days.

Beavers fell trees with their sharp, gnawing teeth. They build dams and lodges (their domelike homes) with the trunks and branches and eat the bark. They store the trees they cut for their winter food supply underwater, near their lodges.

Porcupines munch the bark and twigs of spruce, pine, hemlock, and cottonwood trees. Where do they live? In dens in the ground beneath forests of spruce, pine, hemlock, and cottonwood trees!

Spacious holes in the ground, small spaces beneath rocky overhangs, or hollow logs make fine homes for foxes. Look for traces of fur, feathers, and bones (the remains of recent meals) nearby. A smaller hole surrounded by bits of feathers, fur, and bones is probably the home of a weasel.

Who Is It?

Many mammals are timid and stay out of sight. Though they're hard to spot, a knowing observer (you) can discover a lot about their activities by knowing what signs to look for.

Ever noticed how some of your hair comes out in a comb or brush? You're shedding. Other mammals shed, too. Look for fur caught on a tree branch.

Gnawed bark? High patches are probably porcupines. Shredded bark can be the sign of a bobcat or bear sharpening its claws. Stripped leaves and nipped buds might mean hungry deer.

Look for faint pathways through the trees that border a wooded slope. These are game trails, probably made by deer. Look for their hoof prints wherever the ground is bare and soft.

Most of the holes you see in woods, fields, yards, and city parks are doorways to animal dens. The larger the hole, the larger the animal is likely to be.

Small holes that are hidden by logs often belong to chipmunks. Porcupine and skunk dens are larger. Both of these mammals venture out after dark. If you think you've found one of their holes, ask an adult to hide, wait, and watch for the owner with you after the sun goes down.

Somewhere in the woods, fields, or parks near your home is a stream, creek, pond, or swamp where wild creatures quench their thirst. The damp banks of watering places collect the paw and hoofprints of many mammals.

Many mammals that once lived just in the wilds have moved to towns and cities—coyotes, foxes, badgers, and beavers, to name a few.

ACTIVITY:

Look for animal tracks anywhere there is soft ground or mud (after a rain is a good time to look). Measure both front and back tracks, and compare them to the pictures. Any matches?

Measure the distance between tracks. Which part of the foot made each track? Can you tell if the animal was walking or running?

Do you see the same track in large and small versions? (Could be a mother and baby.)

Follow a set of tracks and you might find an animal's home.

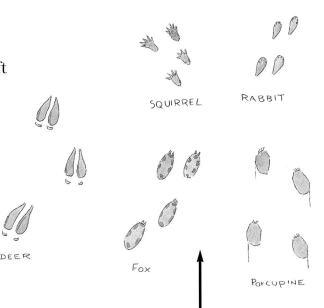

SQUIRREL   RABBIT

DEER

FOX

PORCUPINE

ACTIVITY: Footprints Forever

You can make raised plaster molds of some of the tracks you find, the same way detectives used to make molds of shoe prints at the scene of a crime.

You'll need a cup of plaster of paris, water, a mixing container, something to stir with, a strip of thin cardboard 3 inches wide and 12 inches long, a few paper clips, an old spoon, and a newspaper.

Look for a clear, fully formed track. Bend the cardboard strip into a circle around it, fastening the ends together with paper clips. Press the circled strip firmly into the ground.

Add water to the plaster, a little bit at a time. Stir until it's evenly mixed and about as thick as pancake batter.

Over 3,500 different species of mammals live in America. Although some are found only in certain areas, you can track all of the above mammals in all 50 states. Many are as common in the city as in the country.

43

Slowly pour this mixture inside the circle of cardboard. Let it harden and dry for fifteen minutes. Then lift it from underneath with the help of an old spoon or trowel. Wrap it in newspaper to carry home.

Let it dry in the sun for two hours. Wash it with water and an old toothbrush.

Mammal Miscellaneous

• A prairie dog is not a dog. It's a rodent.

• Whales aren't fish. Mama whales feed their babies milk from their own bodies. That makes them mammals.

• Female opossums can give birth to more than 20 babies at a time, so tiny they can all fit into a single teaspoon.

Your Turn: Bigger Critters
Make your own miscellaneous notes about mammals here.

For the Birds

- Birds are the only living creatures with feathers.

- Bats aren't birds; they have wings, but no feathers.

- Bald eagles aren't bald. Their heads are covered with white feathers.

- Migrating geese can fly at speeds of 65 miles per hour.

Bantamweight

Birds couldn't fly if they weren't so lightweight. They have fewer joints than people have, which means fewer heavy muscles (joints can't be moved without muscles). Their bones are partly hollow and filled with air. In fact, a bird's bones usually weigh less than its feathers.

The golden eagle, a huge bird whose wings stretch 6 feet across when open, weighs only 8 1/2 pounds.

Feather Facts

Birds have three different kinds of feathers. Next to the skin is the bird's "underwear," soft fluffy down that keeps it warm. On top of that are slightly larger "contour" feathers that give the bird shape and color. The stemlike part of the feather is called the shaft. The vane grows from both sides of the shaft at an angle. Contour feathers have thicker shafts and flat tips but are downy at the base. Finally come the big, flat, wing and tail feathers.

Even birds that can't fly, like ostriches and penguins, have feathers.

ACTIVITY:

Spring and summer are the best seasons for finding feathers.

Look for feathers by pools and puddles where birds bathe and preen and near clusters of trees and bushes that birds brush against while flying.

Try to tear a wing or tail feather. See how strong it is? Bend it until the point touches the wide end of the shaft. It's flexible and won't break.

Wing feathers have more vane on one side of the shaft than the other. Tail feathers have shafts right in the middle.

Study it with a magnifying glass. Each vane is made up of hundreds of barbs. Each barb is edged with barbules. The barbules of one barb lock into the barbules of the next barb, sort of like the teeth of a zipper.

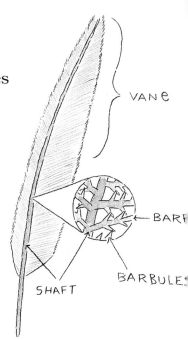

VANE

BARB

BARBULES

SHAFT

WING FEATHER

"Unzip" the barbs of your feather by slowly pulling them toward the thicker end of the shaft. Swish the feather through the air. Does the air flow smoothly across it? Would you depend on a feather like this to carry you high above the treetops? Neither would a bird.

Because birds can't fly without well-groomed, "zipped-up" feathers, they spend lots of time preening.

Now "preen" the feather by smoothing the barbs from the shaft outward. See how the barbs catch and grip each other, making the feather whole again? Swish it through the air once more. Feel the difference?

46

Even well-preened feathers eventually wear out. When this happens, they fall out, and new ones grow in. This is called "molting."

Most birds shed their flight feathers in twos—one from the left and one from the right—so their flying balance won't be affected. They lose just one pair at a time so they don't have to stop flying.

But some, like geese, lose them all at once. They have to keep to the water and be ready to hide until the new set of feathers comes in.

Most and Least: Over 26,000 feathers have been counted on a single whistling swan. Only 940 were counted on a ruby-throated hummingbird. Sparrows have between 2,000 and 3,000.

ACTIVITY:

Find a comfortable place to silently "perch" while you look and listen for birds. How many different kinds of birds can you see?

Look for a robin. Watch it tilt its head to one side. What's it doing? Listening for worms moving underground. Keep watching. Sooner or later it will poke its beak into a hole and pull out a worm!

The EAR-ly bird really does get the worm!

In what ways are airplanes and birds built alike? Are all birds' wings the same shape? Do all birds spend the same amount of time flapping their wings? Gliding? How do birds with short, wide wings fly differently from birds with long, thin wings? Can you tell what kind of wing shapes help a bird fly faster and make sharper turns? Record your observations in **Your Turn**.

Don't waste your time looking for a bird's ears. They're hidden by feathers.

Do you see any birds that look like they're flying just for fun?

(Crows are known for their aerial antics.)

Are We There Yet?

Imagine you are a hummingbird living in northern Montana. Lush, green, mountain valleys are carpeted with an incredible variety of brightly colored wildflowers. The air is crisp, clear, and clean. You have a comfortable nest with a view that seems to go on forever, high on a lofty branch of a cherry tree. The sun shines brightly each day, interrupted only by brief, refreshing, after-noon showers.

Birds (such as nuthatches) that eat seeds usually head north first, followed by insect-eating birds (such as robins). Why? Because seeds are available before insects are. Bluejays, cardinals, and many other birds never migrate at all.

There's just one problem: winter. Every fall, the fruit trees lose their leaves and all the flowers wither and die. Bitter, icy winds sweep down from the north, and snow covers the frozen ground.

What's a hummingbird to do? Migrate.

Many birds fly hundreds, even thousands, of miles south when winter locks their food supply in cold storage. In spring, they backtrack to their rich summer homes, find mates, establish territories, build or rebuild nests, lay eggs, and raise babies.

Some birds return to build nests in the exact same tree year after year.

Do You Eat Like a Bird?

Let's hope not! Food is the fuel that keeps birds flying—and they need a bunch of it. Adult birds eat food weighing half their body weight each day. What do you weigh? 70, 80, or 90 pounds? Imagine downing 35 to 45 pounds (that's 160 dips of ice cream, 100 apples, or 40 loaves of bread) each day!

ACTIVITY:

Make a simple bird table. Ask an adult to help you nail a wooden tray (a flat piece of wood fenced with narrow strips to keep food from falling off) on top of a wooden post. The table will be easier to clean if you leave gaps in the fencing.

Watch the birds feed, and answer these questions:

Which birds are bossy? Which will share? Which fly boldly to the feeder? Which flit around, closer and closer, before finally landing? Which come alone? Which in groups?

A bird's beak is suited to the particular kind of food its species naturally eats—seeds, berries, insects, worms, fish, small mammals, or even other birds. A hawk's sharp, hooked beak, for example, is made for tearing and pulling apart the meat of small animals. Woodpeckers reach their long, thin beaks into narrow openings in tree bark in search of their favorite insects.

Why Birds Tune Up

In early spring, male birds sing to attract mates. Once a male and female pair up, they sing a nest-building song. When the nest is built, they sing a warning, stay-out-of-my-territory song. Soon, their new chicks are peeping and squawking, telling mom and dad they're hungry or afraid.

Place all feeders out of reach of neighborhood cats. You don't want your bird feeder to become a cat feeder!

Are you committed? Once you start feeding the birds in your neighborhood, they'll depend on you. Before you start, make a commitment (a sort of promise) to keep feeding them all winter. If you don't, they might die.

Birds can make a feast on things you throw away: stale bread crusts, leftover popcorn, apple cores, fruit peelings, and cooked bacon rind.

Musical Notes

♪ Birds who live in areas with lots of trees and bushes sing more than birds in wide open spaces.

♪ Birds sing more when it's cloudy than when it's sunny.

♪ Robins sing different songs for morning and evening.

♪ Mockingbirds "borrow" songs from other birds. They even mock, or imitate, police sirens, church choirs, and bulldozers!

♪ Geese honk back and forth to each other as they fly.

A male thrush sings to his hen while she sits on their eggs. He stays a short distance away so he won't call attention to the nest.

Snuggling Up

Nests can be found in all shapes, sizes, and places. Although each bird species builds its own style of nest, all nests have this in common: there must be plenty of the right kind of food close by, and chicks must be safe from predators and weather.

• Starlings build nests of straw and grass in tree holes.

• Magpies build large, bowl-shaped nests with arching roofs in treetops.

• Swallows build under bridges and the eaves of houses, garages, and barns.

• Ovenbirds build what look like upside-down tree nests on the forest floor. They slip in and out through a side door.

• Orioles weave deep sacks hung from sturdy tree branches.

• Teaspoon-sized hummingbird nests, made of bits of tree bark, spider webs, and lichen, are often perched on the uppermost branches of fruit trees.

Why don't birds fall off their branches while sleeping? The tendons of their toes lock their grip on the perch. Even when birds relax, their toes stay locked in place.

ACTIVITY:

You can help birds build their nests in spring and summer. Gather paper strips, scraps of aluminum foil, human or animal hair (whatever comes out in a brush after a vigorous combing of you or your pet), bits of cotton or wool material, stuffing from old furniture, small twigs, and leaves. Arrange it all in a mesh bag (the kind grapefruits and oranges are sold in) and hang it from a sturdy tree branch. Many birds also build with mud, so create a small spot of bare, wet ground for them.

MAGPIE NEST

SWALLOW NEST

HUMMINGBIRD NEST

Wait and watch from a spot where the birds can't see you. (Be patient. It may take time for the birds to notice your gift). Note (in **Your Turn**, of course) which birds visit and which materials they choose for their nests. Are there more males or females (the male of a species is frequently brighter in color than the female)? How many trips do they make? Over what period of time? How do the birds use their beaks?

Eggsplorations

All female birds lay eggs. Bird moms, and sometimes dads, sit on the eggs to keep them warm while a chick grows inside.

When a chick is ready to hatch, it punches a hole in the shell with a small spike on the top of its beak called an eggtooth. It then turns around inside the egg, breaking the shell in a line starting at the hole. It pushes and peeps, peeps and pushes, and the crack widens. Finally, the shell splits in two, and a tired but triumphant chick gets its first look at the outside world.

The largest bird nest ever discovered was 9 1/2 feet wide by 20 feet deep and was estimated to weigh more than 4,000 pounds. A pair of bald eagles (possibly aided by their offspring) built, rebuilt, and added onto this same nest over many years.

ACTIVITY:

Crack open a chicken's egg. Feel how strong the shell is? The yellow yolk you see is formed high inside a hen's body. As the yolk moves down a tube through the hen's body, it's covered with albumen (the egg "white") and coated with minerals that will harden into a shell.

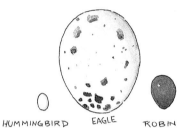

HUMMINGBIRD   EAGLE   ROBIN

When a hen and a rooster mate, the rooster leaves sperm in the part of the hen's body where the yolk is. When the sperm comes in contact with the yolk, a chick is created.

Examine your egg's yolk. If it was bought at a health food store, it may have a tiny red spot, which means the hen and a rooster have mated. The spot is the beginning of a chick. Protein from the yellow yolk will feed it as it develops. The white albumen will protect it.

Sperm + egg = baby chick

The colors of many eggshells protect them by making them hard to see. Blue eggs, for instance, are usually laid by birds that build nests in shady areas.

	Your Turn: For the Birds
○	

Water, Water Everywhere

- Nearly 3/4 of the earth's surface is covered with water.

- Water is one of only a few substances that commonly occurs in all 3 states of matter: solid, liquid, and gas.

- About 2 out of every 100 cups of the earth's water exist as snow or ice.

- More than 95 out of every 100 cups of the earth's water are salty.

- No matter how much water people drink, wash their cars with, flush down their toilets, bathe in, or sprinkle on their lawns, the total amount on earth stays the same.

When the sun heats the water in ponds, lakes, oceans, plants (remember how leaves "perspire" into the air?), or even a pile of wet blankets, some of the water evaporates.

Some water is evaporating all the time. The water in the air is called humidity. Lots of humidity makes you feel sticky on warm, still days.

Air can only hold a certain amount of water vapor. When it's "full," evaporation stops, and the water vapor condenses.

When water evaporates, it changes from a liquid you can drink into a gas (vapor) that you can breathe.

Condensing is the opposite of **vaporizing.** When water vapor condenses, it turns from invisible gas back into a liquid.

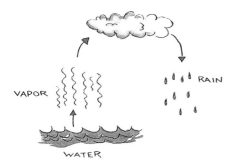

VAPOR

RAIN

WATER

If the air is very cold, it sleets, hails, or snows.

One hot summer day, you may suck on a piece of ice. Some of the liquid from the ice leaves your body as perspiration and evaporates into the air.

Tiny droplets of water join together in the air to form clouds. These drops combine into bigger drops and become too heavy for the clouds to hold. The water falls back to the earth as rain.

Eventually the water from that ice cube returns to earth as rain. It may run off the land into a stream that will carry it to a river that will carry it to a pond, lake, or ocean. When the sun heats the pond, lake, or ocean, some of that same water again evaporates into the air.

Before long, this wandering water returns to the earth as rain. This time, it soaks into the ground and is sucked up by the roots of a tree. When the tree "perspires," the water

_ _ _ _ _ _ _ _ _ _ .

Soon the _ _ _ _ _ returns to the _ _ _ _ _ as _ _ _ _ . And so on and so on . . .

 ACTIVITY:

Take a spring or summer walk in the rain. Smell the plants and soil. Feel the rain on your nose and eyelashes. Listen to the different sounds rain-drops make when they land on leaves, rocks, branches, roofs, and YOU. Notice how the water rolls off various types of leaves. Examine a raindrop through a

magnifying glass. Describe what you smell, see, feel, and hear in **Your Turn**.

Don't forget to check the sky for a rainbow when the sun comes out!

ACTIVITY: Rain Gauging

Make a rain gauge so you can track rainfall in your area. First, cut the top 5 inches off an empty, clear, 1-liter, plastic soda bottle (ask an adult to help). Set the bottle neck in the bottle base, like a funnel. Use a ruler and permanent marker to put 1/16-, 1/8-, 1/4-, and 1/2-inch measurements on the bottle.

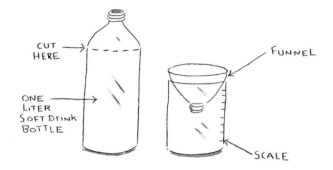

Place the rain gauge out in the open where rainwater will fall straight into it. Do not place it where water can run into it from the leaves of a tree or the eaves of a building. Place bricks or rocks around the base so it won't blow over.

Record the date and amount of every rainfall in **Your Turn**.

Frog Facts

The first warm spring rains bring pond creatures to life. "Spring's on the way!" peep the tiny frogs known as spring peepers. You can hear them a mile away. When you get close, they hush all at once.

WHAT ANIMAL OUTDOES A CAT WITH 9 LIVES?

A frog—because he croaks every night.

You're not likely to see them. Peepers are no larger than a nickel and thoroughly blend in with their surroundings.

- Amphibians (animals such as frogs and toads that live both on land and in water) have been on earth longer than any living creatures.

- Peepers can jump 17 times their body length. That's like you leaping from one end of a basketball court to the other.

- Most frogs hatch, mate, and lay their eggs in water.

- Frogs "reel in" insects with their long tongues.

- Female frogs can lay 250,000 eggs in their lives (but fish gobble most of them).

- Male frogs croak to attract females. Most frogs croak slowly when it's cold and faster when it's warm.

• Are you reminded of crickets?

- Some frogs live for 30 or 40 years.

- Tadpoles and pollywogs are the same thing.

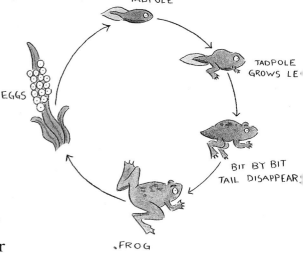

TADPOLE

TADPOLE GROWS LE

BIT BY BIT TAIL DISAPPEAR

FROG

EGGS

Frog eggs hatch into tiny tadpoles in a wee or so. At first they live off the yolk inside their bodies, but soon they're munching on water plants. Next they grow back legs and then tiny front ones. Bit by bit their tails d appear, and they swim to the surface for a first breath of air.

56

ACTIVITY: Don't drink the water!

Fill a bucket with water from a pond. Place it where it won't be disturbed. Does the water look different after 5 minutes?

Because pebbles, sand, plants, and dirt have settled to the bottom, the water looks much cleaner. However, it's still full of floating bacteria and rotting plant and animal parts that can't be seen without a microscope.

Here's how you can clean that water up:

Wash and dry a clay flower pot. Set it in a clear container.

Line the pot with paper coffee filters. Fill 1/3 of it with small pieces of charcoal. Add well-rinsed sand until the pot is 2/3 full. Fill the rest of the pot with rinsed gravel.

Now slowly pour the pond water through the mesh strainer into the pot. The biggest particles will be trapped in the strainer. Material small enough to make it through the strainer but large enough to be easily seen will be caught by the gravel. Material small enough to flow through the gravel but too large to flow through the sand will be trapped there. The charcoal and filter paper will catch and hold the smallest matter.

Now compare water straight from the pond, water from the top of the bucket (after settling), and the water seeping through the coffee filter into the clear container under the pot.

First rinse the sand and gravel in a fine-mesh strainer until the water running through is clear.

PAPER COFFEE FILTER

STRAINER

POT

LARGE CLEAR CONTAINER

SAND

CHARCOAL

GRAVEL

57

The filtered water appears quite clean. Still, there are thousands of invisible germs. Even one sip could make you very sick.

Pond Habitats

A pond provides four different and distinct habitats.

First is the shoreline. Look for salamanders in the cool damp mud, darting minnows and tadpoles hiding among the shallow water plants, and water birds that build nests in the shoreline foliage.

The top of the water, the second habitat, is home to a variety of insects and floating plants.

The third habitat, the open water, supports turtles, amphibians, water mammals (such as beavers), still more insects, and an amazing variety of fish.

Finally, the pond's bottom nurtures worms, clams, and more insect larvae.

Fish Facts

Almost all fish are a brownish green color from above. This keeps them from being easily seen by predators (including humans with fishing poles). You might be surprised at the bright colors that flash from their sides and bellies underwater.

- Many fish eat their own babies. Still, the different species survive because so many thousands of eggs are laid.

- Some fish swim slowly by rowing with their fins. Most, however, propel themselves through the water by swishing their tails back and forth.

- When water temperatures drop in the winter, fish become inactive. As temperatures rise, their activity levels heat up.

- Many fish species are almost impossible for humans to tell apart. Fish don't have that problem. They recognize and breed only within their species.

The Birth and Death of a Pond

When beavers build dams of crisscrossed sticks, stones, and plastered mud across a stream, the water is trapped and a pond is born. Beavers build their lodges, complete with underwater entrances, in such ponds from trees they cut down with their teeth. Eager beavers can down a 5-inch diameter tree in 30 minutes.

Before long, reeds and rushes begin to grow around the shoreline. Fish swim downstream into the pond. A redwing blackbird lands in search of food for his dinner. Ducks and geese build nests in the rushes. Frogs and toads arrive to mate and lay eggs. Insect larvae hatch on top of the calm water. Elk leave the shelter of the nearby trees to drink from the pond. Raccoons wash their food in it. All kinds of creatures, from near and far, like what they see at the pond and stay.

As the weeks and months pass, the stream carries sand and soil into the pond. Some of it settles to the bottom. When the plants and animals that live in the pond die, they, too, sink to the bottom. Over the years, layers of sand and soil, dead plants, and decaying animal matter accumulate, or pile up, and the pond fills in and grows shallow. Plants at the edge grow toward the middle, and the pond becomes narrow. The beavers, who have used all the nearby trees for building and eating, move away in search of a new home that has trees aplenty.

With no busy beavers to repair it, the dam begins to leak. Heavy rains swell the stream and part of the dam washes away. What remains of the pond pours out, and the pond soon disappears.

The land, however, has become extremely fertile. New plants begin to sprout from the rich soil. Soon it will be a lush meadow, a birthplace to many new plants, animals, and insects.

Your Turn: Water, Water Everywhere

A Challenge to Naturalist-Explorers

Our planet is in trouble.

Many lakes, rivers, and oceans are polluted. Much of the air we breathe is no longer clean. Whole forests are chopped down every day to meet demands for lumber and paper goods. Wild animal habitats are being replaced by golf courses and malls. Chemicals from factories and car exhaust dissolve in water and create acid rain. Landfills are overflowing with nonbiodegradable garbage and poisonous waste. The gas, oil, and coal that are burned for fuels release carbon dioxide into the air, causing a global warming effect.

Give a Gift to Nature

What will happen to our planet is partly your responsibility. You have a choice to make: you can be a part of the problem or part of the solution.

How can you help? It's as simple as this: Don't waste things such as food, fuel, paper, or water. Buy products that are made from biodegradable materials. Recycle glass, paper, and cardboard packaging. Repair possessions instead of throwing them away. Don't litter or pollute. Avoid using products that contain harmful chemicals.

When something is biodegradable, it can be harmlessly broken down and returned to the earth.

Although the United States is home to only 6% of the world's population, it uses 40% of its resources.

ACTIVITY:

Begin a list in **Your Turn** of ways you and your family can help save the Earth. Here are some suggestions to get you started:

- **Walk, bike, or carpool whenever possible.**
- **Ask for grocery sacks made of paper instead of plastic.**
- **Don't buy things you don't really need.**
- Separate aluminum cans, glass bottles and jars, plastic containers, and newspapers from the rest of your family's garbage. Take them to a recycling center.
- **Turn off lights and water faucets when not needed.**
- **Never throw away clothes, books, and toys. Pass them along to someone who can use them.**
- Avoid styrofoam containers and cups and disposable plastic dishes.
- **Pack lunch foods and drinks in reusable containers.**

Celebrate Life

Now is a good time to read back over all the journal entries you've made in the **Your Turn** pages. Have you learned anything about nature? Do you see some of nature's details more clearly?

This book is just a first step in celebrating life, which is, after all, a special occasion each and every day.

Your Turn: Ways to Save the Earth

Index